The Hippopotamus
THESAURUS
A Menagerie of Delectable Words
HEFTY

VOLUME 1.

written & illustrated by
Samuel Jennings Vinson

R&S
R&Stone

An Imprint of R & Stone House *Publishing*

The HIPPOPOTAMUS THESAURUS

A Hefty Menagerie of Delectable Words

VOLUME 1.

In this book is an umpteen of some of the most delicious, *real* words I could find for you. Words that are fun to look at and even more thrilling to say.

In the following pages are words that will tickle the tongue, twist your noggin, chuckle your laugh-box with oodles and googles for the noodles of young pupils.

Find a comfy nook and snack by yourself or find someone to read to, for some words are best served aloud.

Grab a spoon (*or ladle*), and dig in with me!

don't forget to check the glossary!

Library of Congress Cataloging-in-Publication Data is available.
Library of Congress Control Number: 2024915015
ISBN 979-8-9907024-4-8

Design & Illustration by Samuel Jennings Vinson

-

First Edition

For all teachers.

Whether it be schoolteachers, parents, siblings, mentors, or anything in between, this book is dedicated to those that share everything they have to foster the brilliance of young minds.

Don't read this book.

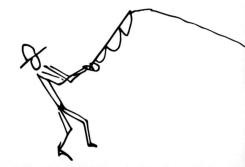

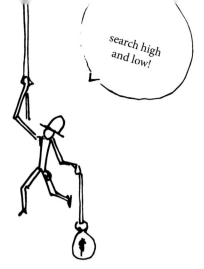

Explore it.

BUMFUZZLE
/BUM-fuh-zuhl/

A curious sprite, a hungry little beast.
Between the pages of our books,
he lives,
and *feasts*.

You cannot see him for in the pages he snuzzles,
chomping at words, he nustles and guzzles.

The Bumfuzzle lives in the books with big words,
the delectable homonyms, the transitive verbs.

Small as the dust that adorns the books' covers,
he nibbles and searches,
for words with the most colors.

When we're not looking,
when he's selected his treat,
he grows as big as can be, so our books he can eat.

We know not much of this mysterious creature.
All we know, is that he longs for a teacher.

He looks for the words he has yet to understand,
to dispel his confusion, for his mind to expand.

It is said though he reads,
he is a great listener,
that he longs to be taught,
for your words to hear.

Next time you find a word
that makes your head
scratch and puzzle,
read it aloud, to our friend,
Bumfuzzle.

WAMBLE

/WAM-buhl/

A growly old geezer,
a rightful old tart.

A grumbling gudgeon,
a blabbering blart.

He sits in our tummy banging his drum,
louder and louder,
when the food there is none.

This dastardly nuisance,
we call him a Wamble.
For when we are hungry,
he is a fierce little mongrel.

You must tell your parents,
there's only one way to appease him.

You must serve him dessert,
or things could get grim...

11

DISCOMBOBULATED
/dis-kum-BOB-yuh-lated-ed/

A long time ago,
there was a tribe of Befuddles.
They lived in peace with the Baffles,
they all laughed and they chuckled.

One day from the wilderness a Flummox appeared,
a michevious imp with a purpley beard.

He came with a mission to impart a confusion,
so the Befuddles and Baffles could not draw a conclusion.

From the stump of the Boggle Tree in the middle of town,
his little hooves stood firm, "ALL YE, GATHER ROUND!"

He says to the crowd, "I ask you this, my impossible question.."
winking and grinning with michevious expression.

"If you butter toast and tie to a cat's back,
which side will land first,
the cat's paws or the snack?"

The Befuddles exclaimed,
"If you drop buttered toast it will *always* land top side down!

To which the Baffles replied,
"The *cat* will always land on its feet,
don't be such a clown!"

Back and forth they went, the Befuddles and Baffles,
and the Flummox he chuckled, giggled and cackled.

To this day they've been stuck,
for years they've debated.

To this day they remain,
discombobulated.

13

BODACIOUS
/boh-DAY-shuhs/

About seven-foot-three with a jawline of marble,
he can juggle three cows *with* a 500 lb. barbell.

A sideshow performer, he travels with the circus,
everyone marvels, but they don't know his true purpose.

In his caravan he shines, away from the rabble,
he's picked up a hobby, in French cooking he dabbles.

Cassoulets and ragout, foi gras with bordeaux,
he confies blackened garlic, he prepares escargot.

Nimble and swift (though cramped in his small kitchen),
each dish he prepares, they shimmer and glisten.

Today is his favorite, Beef Bourguignon:
steak braised in red wine, with herbs that he's grown.

He must eat by himself for he knows his true skill,
if he told any others, his small camper they'd fill.
So in between shows when he's not lifting horses,
he's planning his menu, refining his courses.

Someday, he hopes, when his
circus days are through,
he will start his own restaurant,
in downtown Toulouse.

He can't wait for others
to see him as Chef,
to look past his good looks
and to see him as Jeff.

Even though he is
irresistable and very
flirtatious,
a little conceited
with a dash of audacious,
there is only one thing where
he's truly tenacious.

That's to be seen as Chef Jeff,
and not just bodacious.

ONOMATOPOEIA
/AH-nuh-MAH-tuh-PEE-uh/

Chickadee chirps with a tweet and a cheep,
"Chicka-dee-dee-dee!" as she flutters,
with a swoosh and beep.

Cuckoo Bird pops with the whirr of the clock
"Cuckoo-Cuckoo!" he honks,
with a pop and a gawk.

Hippopotamus plops into the pool
with a splish and a splash,
the whole ground rumbles with a glorious crash.
He wants to have a sound that is just like "ACHOO!"
but he doesn't meow, ribbit, or moo.

"Hippo-Hippo!"

Theodore says as an idea,
but wait that doesn't work,
that's not an onomatopoeia..

POTTLE
/POT-ul/

Grandmother Glormp's Glorious Gumbread

2 cups of flour
1 inklebird egg
1 cup of sugar
2 tablespoons of vanilla extract
1 cup of used bubblegum *(the best ones are found under the desk of the boy who blows bubbles in class that pop and stick to his chin, you know who he is)*
1/4 pottle of bluttergoat milk

Step 1: Wash hands. Preheat oven to 350 degrees.

Step 2: Mix inklebird egg, sugar, vanilla extract.

Step 3: Chew bubblegum until tender (you'll know when you can blow a bubble),
and mix evenly into batter.

Step 4: Slowly add flour and bluttergoat milk,
1/16th a pottle at a time.
Put in oven for 347-402 seconds.

Step 5: Let cool for 0.27 hours.

Bon apetit!

how much is a pottle?

NIFF
/nif/

Phew! Oh my, what a pungent aroma!
If I take a deep breath I'll fall into a coma!

It smells like the back side of a wet warthog,
(*not that I know what that smells like...*)
I wish my nose was stuffy, that it was clogged!

It smells like a bungle of Phuuts in a bucket,
you can smell it from here all the way to Nantucket!

Like a whole twizzle of Funkus mixed with old socks,
like a blumbering herd of Bestunkles,
all crammed in a box!

There *has* to be a word for it, this terrible sniff...
Oh, here it is in the dictionary,
they call it, a "niff."

18

FLOUNCE
/flowns/

How boring! How dull!
How quite so drab.
To just bump in the night,
it lacks the gift of The Gab.

We do much more whilst you young ones are sleeping.
We slink and we pounce, we saunter while creeping!

We jump and we slump, we crump with our rumps!
We sashay and we boogie, we twizzle and thump!

We scuttle and scamper, we hop with our paws,
We scramble and shuffle, (though we did break Mom's vase.)

We zig and we zag, we waltz and we wiggle,
We zip and we zoom, we skitter and jiggle!

There is one word
that brings me delight,
for I don't just bump,
I *flounce* in the night.

19

QUIXOTIC
/kwik-SOT-ik/

wait, thats not a real bird, maybe there's another one around here.

Come hither and gawk,
come gather and wonder,
feast your eyes on my plumage,
there's only ONE of *ME* in the flock.

How strange, you must think,
to see such a spectacle,
I assure you it's real,
no need to be skeptical.

Not quite what you'd expect,
from a bird of my stature,
I'm one of a kind,
to never be captured.

Some might see me as dreamy,
maybe foolish or silly,
I prefer audacious,
I'm so cool I'm chilly.

I'm one of a kind
with colors hypnotic,
A new species of bird,
The Long-Tailed Quixotic.

BIBLIOPOLE
/BIB-lee-uh-pohl/

Welcome my dear, to Fred's Fantastical Folios,
We have Romeo, Othello, Frodo, Pinocchio.

Beowulf, Illiad, Anna Karenina, Dickens and Poe,
The Great Gastby, Don Quixote, even Thoreau.

Be careful, don't touch, these are exceedingly rare,
the pages are old so they could easily tear.

This is the FIRST copy of Pride and Prejudice,
it's worth more than a unicorn, I'll tell you this..

This leather binding is almost 500 years old,
it's The Canterbury Tales, even gilded with gold.

Each book has a story, beyond what's just in the pages,
they've been tested by time, loved through the ages.

Every member of this collection is near and dear to my soul,
it's my passion and life's work, to be a bibliopole.

21

CRYPTIC
/krip-tick/

A winding road,
a perilous trek.

21 steps to complete it,
each page you must check.

This might be the beginning,
or just the middle.

If you complete the loop,
you are the master of riddles.

let's skedaddle!

HIPPOPOTOMONSTROSESQUIPPEDALIOPHOBIA
/hip-uh-pot-uh-mon-stroh-ses-kwip-uh-dal-ee-uh-foh-bee-uh/

Help!
A monster!
It has teeth made of letters!
It's gotten too large,
it's ruffled my feathers!

I am but a wee thing,
only small things I say.
My life is simple,
and I like it that way.

I do not like words that are more than a bite,
more than a few letters *surely* gives me a fright.

Don't make me, I'm scared,
this gives not a BIT of euphoria..

Ok fine, I'll try...

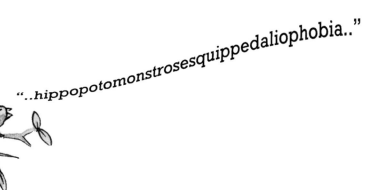

"..hippopotomonstrosesquippedaliophobia.."

25

ENIGMA
/uh-nig-muh/

Every story we have has a nugget of truth,
yet there are fables we know from our earliest youth.

Never once do we question why we feel someone is snooping,
or why water only boils when we are not looking.

I challenge you this: find the answers between,
find the real meaning, the one that's unseen.

Go forth in the dark, between the shadows and you,
uncover the treasure of, "what is deja vu?"

Mark your steps and leave breadcrumbs for the path it is winding,
if you peer too far into mystery you could regret what you're finding..

A tip for explorers who seek that dim signal,
just read each other line, you'll find the enigma.

QUOMODOCUNQUIZE
/kwuh-moh doh-kuhn-kwahyz/

Stop on by, peruse my collection,
everything here is for sale, without an exception.

I must be clear, everything here has a price,
no freebies here, not even the ice.

The lemonade is a quarter,
the cup is a dime,
I also charge for the straw,
and that isn't a crime.

My younger brother doesn't know it,
but I'll offer you his service.
It's two dollars per lawn mowed,
and I will take half of each purchase.

Um excuse me, how dare you have the audacity!
Picking flowers on my lawn?!
Even after my hospitality?!

That will be two nickels, please.
No, you can't give them back.
You've already picked them,
put your coins in my sack.

You might think I'm a Scrooge
but I'm really just wise,
I make money
any way possible,
I quomodocunquize.

Lemonade: 25¢
+ Cup: 10¢
+ Straw: 5¢

27

HULLABALOO
/huh-luh-BAH-loo/

The elephants trumpet,
make thunder with hooves,
they bellow and bluster,
to show they disapprove.

The monkeys all hoot,
then the hollers ensue,
they swing from the trees,
they all fling their .. shoes.

The buffalo rumble,
they move with such speed,
huffing and bumbling,
a stinky stampede.

The flamingos revolt,
a rowdy feathered parade,
they screech and they squawk,
a hot pink brigade.

Even the rabbits have joined in the tussle,
to show they can also cause chaos,
even if just a rustle.

The panda however,
calmly nibbles bamboo.
He thinks to himself,
"Why all the hullabaloo?"

COLLYWOBBLE
/KOL-ee-wob-ul/

Do you remember our grumpy old friend,
gurgling Mr. Wamble?

Well, he has quite the family,
a real rumbling ensemble.

A traveling band, they love to make music.
So in our tummies they live,
they find it acoustic.

Rarely do they speak over one another,
they have their own stage times,
and their voices do smother.

I'll tell you of Wamble's lovely young sister,
she only sings loud,
when our stomach's a twister.

When we're in the back seat and our stomach is queasy,
she bangs on her xylophone,
until we are wheezy.

With our hands on our bellies,
when we only can waddle,
say hello to the
boisterous,
rambunctious,
unruly,
Ms. Collywobble.

DYSANIA
/di-SAY-nee-uh/

I urge you please, you must find me a doctor,
a physician, a shrink, a potion concocter.

Anything, really, I'm in dire straits,
I can reach out to touch them,
those pearled Heaven's Gates.

I promise you, I mean it,
I'm surely not bluffing,
these blankets are too heavy,
it's like lead, all this fluffing.

Tell my teachers farewell,
for I'll (almost) miss their homework.
I promise you, I mean it,
I'm not trying to shirk.

It's a condition you see,
a real one in fact.
I can't get out of bed,
even if just for a nap.

A serious malady,
it is not just some mania.
Look it up, I dare you,
I've contracted Dysania.

DOCTOR NOTE:
NO School
=
Treatment:
Unlimited
dollops of
ICE CREAM
Doctor

31

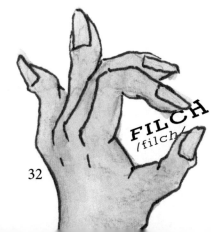

FILCH
/filch/

DOOZY
/DOO-zee/

Little Suzie was quite choosy,
"Not this, not that,"
until she was woozy.

She always got her way,
for she was quite schmoozy,
"I only like donuts and smoothies and sushi."

One day they ran out of her favorite treats,
and she found herself hungry, with nothing to eat.

"Oh what shall I do, maybe I am too bougie,
this is a pickle, I'm in such a *doozy*!"

METHINKS
/me-THINKS/

Maybe,
perhaps,
anyways, well humph..
I'm not quite sure,
I just might be stumped.

Is it this foot?
No, that foot!

I just cannot tell,
where my toes I should park.
Maybe,
methinks,
I shouldn't put my shoes on in the dark.

BIBBLE
/BIB-ul/

Manners, please,
do not speak and chew.
It is quite rude,
when your dinner gets spewed.

Be polite with your volume,
there's others around us.
If they were to yell,
it surely would drown us.

Use your napkin,
your chin has a dribble,
just try please,
to not be such a Bibble.

35

GUMNIVOROUS
/guhm-NIV-er-ruhs/

If you have a question, please make it quick.
I'm in the best part of dessert,
so let me please lick.

All this tree's sap, so oozy and juicy,
if I could, I would,
fill an entire jacuzzi.

I'm a Fork-marked lemur, all I dine on is sap,
I eat til I'm full, then I have a nice nap.

I do not like veggies,
fried okra, potatoes,
fish-sticks or ice cream,
    not even chicken alfredo.

I do not like fettucine,
    tortellini, not even paninis,
        burritos or tacos,
            linguine, zucchini.

Not even gazpacho paired
with some nachos,
    or a plate of hot waffles
    topped with falafel.

So if you would please,
    bump your rump along that way,
    I have a nap to attend to,
        and it shall not delay.

36

WIDDERSHINS
/WID-er-shinz/

The clockmaker sits with his head in his hands,
surrounded by cogs, watches, wristbands.

"Why won't you work, why do you continue to mock?"
He says to the clock that just won't tick-tock.

"Backwards, am I, ookcuc, ookcuc!"
Replies the clock when the twelve it has struck.

"Forwards go cannot I,
tock-tick, tock-tick!"
As the big hand moves
backwards to quarter til six.

"Wise clock counter, am I,"
it says as the hands spin,
 "Eureka!"
the clockmaker exclaims with a grin.

He rustles for tools,
some cogwheels and pins,
"I'll fix you up,
you're just widdershins!"

FLIBBERTIGIBBET
/FLIB-er-tee-JIB-it/

We all know of the frog that when kissed turns to a prince,
there's another one like him, if you'll let me convince.

A little bit different, and not quite so charming,
some find her obnoxious, even alarming.

In the forests of Scotland, there's a wee lass,
she lives in the bushes, brambles and grass.

Rarely seen by our eyes yet we know that she's there,
for she's always talking, she's full of hot air.

About three inches tall, weighs less than an ounce,
she looks like a mixture of toad, bird, and mouse.

She's a talented vocalist, a prolific, adept mimic,
she has us all fooled with her tricks and her gimmicks.

She never stops talking but has dozens of voices,
she has so many to pull from, so many choices.

She can throw her voice far, to every small nook,
she can sound like a sparrow, or bubbling brook.

She's been known to copy the sound of children's laughter,
then giggles herself, when we all run after.

Sometimes she likes to make the telephone ring,
but no one is calling, she just likes to sing.

Only *one* species is known to be able to find her,
only the house cat can see this mysterious speaker.

When your cat zooms all of a sudden and FLIES through the room,
she's probably found something, and now you know whom.

If you ever hear something out of place like a ribbit,
there's an awfully good chance, it's a Flibbertigibbet.

CANOODLE
/kuh-NOO-duhl/

I can never resist...
your slobbery kiss,
each lick is such bliss.

I'll take all of it, the whole kit and caboodle,
I can't say no, if I tried it'd be futile.

Give me more, don't be frugal
I just want your love,
your whiskered approval.

There isn't anyone else I'd rather canoodle,
besides you, good girl,
my fluffy old poodle.

VAMOOSE
/vuh-MOOS/

HEY! how many points on these antlers?

If I could only choose an excuse,
yet I have no alibis to produce...

I'm not cowardly, wimpy, lily-livered or frail,
but he's coming up on us,
we should turn tail!

The fact of the matter is I am just frightened,
I have to admit,
my tushy is tightened.

Who knew the zoo had a moose on the loose?!
I think we should run,
we gotta vamoose!

SCUTTLEBUTT
/SKUT-ul-but/

Quiver me fingers, why's it always, "AHOY?"
We've plundered the dictionary,
there be more words we enjoy...

If me hear, "Yar, matey," one more time I'll jump off the plank,
there be dullards among us, their word banks are blank.

We're raiders and rovers, malfactors, and pilferers,
yet to the term, "pirate," we be held prisoner.

We canvass the seas, traverse the horizon,
my crew be not learners, they might never wizen.

There be one mate who has a wee bit of promise,
he don't miss a word, I guarantee this.

He noses our business, a real gossipy mutt.
There be no other word,
he's a right Scuttlebutt.

SNOLLYGOSTER
/SNOH-lee-gaw-ster/

At 100 pounds and 0.89 smoots tall,
this little villian shouted in a southeastern drawl,

"I don't care what you need, this is what I want!
I'm immune to your heckles, I can't hear your taunts!"

In front of the assembly he stood, red-faced and puffy,
with oily hair and a belly that's fluffy.

"It's my turn to speak, I'll take all the time that I need,
you'll be here a week in your suits of full tweed.

I have a grievance so large that I won't shut up 'til it's fixed,
It seems ONE of you, maybe two, has stolen my sandwich!
It was *clearly* labeled "Sir Pugel", it was a Reuben on rye.
I'm sure the culprit has sauce on their fingers,
everyone raise their hands to the sky!"

"We shall do none of the sort," said Honorable Judge Shelly Sanders
"We have other things to attend to, much more pressing matters."

The villian huffed and he puffed
and would not get off of the stand,
so the judge ordered the guards,
"Apprehend this small man!"

"This is a place of justice, order,
decorum, and good posture,
you are henceforth dismissed,
you vile snollygoster!"

43

FALLACY

/FAL-uh-see/

Let's play a game, a scholarly duel.
We will both give each other a fact,
our favorite intellectual jewel.

I'm always looking to learn,
my bookworm does thirst.
So give me your best,
alright, you go first.

Holy crumpets that's amazing! Why didn't someone tell me!
Bananas are berries *and* so are kiwi??

Hang on, I will let you go on and wait for my turn,
it seems that from you I have much more to learn...

Well then what other things do I know that actually *are* berries?
Pomegranates, avocados, tomatoes?? Well now I am wary...

What else do I know that has been misconstrued?
What other things have I seen that I've wrongly viewed?
How many berries actually are not, as defined by the library?
Not even strawberries or raspberries or even cherries??

I am bumfuzzled on how much I don't know,
about the things that I did, all the facts that are faux.

I think I will do more research,
on *everything* in my reality,
just to make sure,
that it's not a fallacy.

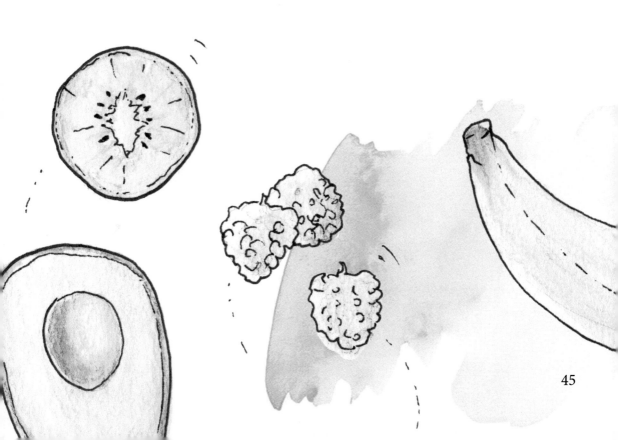

45

PALINDROME
/PAL-in-drohm/

Excuse me please,
do you have a moment, Madam?
Would you like a racecar, or if I may, a yam?

Come browse my wares,
I collect odd things as my job.
You don't have to buy them,
you can borrow or rob.

It's so nice to meet you, my name is Otto,
I'd introduce you to my brother but,
Olson is in Oslo.

I'm afraid I've sold out, I have not a banana baton,
though they do sell those across the street,
at Nola's Salon.

Why yes it is, that is a very rare bird rib,
from the long extinct species, The Bijobojib.

psst!
how many palindromes?
add 6 and go there...

Over there on the shelf by the Pobibop tongue,
I collected it myself, that is Gnu dung.

In the bottled flower section,
don't knock the lid off a daffodil,
it has magical pollen, and one whiff could kill.

All the prices you'll see are imaginary digits to believe in,
for they're numbers, but not, they're never odd or even.

This specimen here I believe was found by a Canadian,
this one is special, this is Neil, an alien.

Thank you for stopping in,
I'm quite glad you did pry.
My favorite dessert is a number,
for I prefer pi.

GORGONZOLA
/gor-guhn-ZOH-luh/

My whooooole life, in all of my years,
there is only *one* thing that will bring me to tears.

The good kind of course,
when our eyes water when happy,
(and I'm not a crier, this is not to be sappy).

I want to tell you
what makes me weak in the knees,
it's that ooey, that gooey,
that wonderful cheese.

Camembert and cheddar,
Roquefort and Manchego,
I challenge you,
to find me a cheese I don't know.

Taleggio, chèvre, our lovely burrata,
mozzarella on tomatoes,
feta (and honey) on foccacia.

Next time you invite me to a tea party
for a delightful affair,
I shall be woefully disappointed, if
there is no Gruyère.

I do not want crackers,
please hold the granola,
just give me a wheel,
of well-aged gorgonzola.

PETRICHOR
/PET-ri-kor/

The desert toad slumbers, deep in the soil.
In the shade of the yucca the lizards' tails coil.

It's been a long and hot summer for the clouds have withheld,
many months have passed by since the rivers have swelled.

The roadrunner flits between the shade of the brush,
the stink bug lumbers onward without a care or a rush.

Something is different about the shape of the clouds,
they have a flat belly beneath the dark that enshrouds.

Even the wind has begun to inquire,
whispering gently of what's soon to transpire.

The prairie dogs poke their heads out of their homes,
curious sniffles at the earth's new cologne.

Everyone bustles for cover in hurried excitement,
they know what this smell means before thunder,
when it is most quiet.

The pitter patter starts, the clouds open and pour,
all the animals rejoice at the smell,
at last, petrichor.

ICHTHYOCOPROLITE
/ik-thee-oh-KOP-ruh-lyt/

I've done it, I'm famous! This rock must be worth millions!
I'll sell it to the museum for trillions and zillions!

I can tell that it's old, probably from the Triassic,
that's at *least* 30 MILLION years before the Jurassic.

Lucky for me, I have a paleontologist uncle,
he just got back from a dig in the Amazon jungle.

Yes, there *were* dinosaurs there and he just proved it,
It's called, "*Amazonsaurus maranhensis*", from the preamazonic.

I can't wait to see him to show him my find,
I know that it's special, it's one of a kind.

Finally I can show him and give him my treasure,
I can't wait to be rich, forever and ever.

"Well," he says with his eyes on a loupe,
"It's ichthyocoprolite,
just fossilized fish poop."

VOODOO
/VOO-doo/

glossary

Who knew our thoughts flew,
they zoom on through,
and choo-choo to you.

If you give it, you get it,
even yahoos and thank yous.
So be careful to only wish onto others,
true views and good news.

Here, you can try,
here's something to chew:
give a hug to your bear,
Mr. Blue Bearstein Baloo.

Be sure you imbue a smooch,
or, maybe two,
and wish that it lands somewhere other than you.

It's true,
what you spew does accrue.
So make it all love,
and what ensues is Good Voodoo.

MAGNAMINITY
/mag-nan-IM-i-tee/

"What a manificent find," the great grey shrike muses,
 I do hope she likes it and it's me that she chooses.

I am a bit hungry but this big worm is for her,
I know she will like it, of this I am sure."

"What else can I bring that will catch her attention?",
the great grey shrike thinks with great apprehension.

"See look at me, I'm unlike the others!
I want to give you the world,
the things with most colors!"

You see, it's in his nature to be incredibly generous,
he will go to great lengths, for he is adventurous.

There's a nugget of wisdom to take from the shrike,
you give your heart to others,
even if you're not alike.

It comes with practice and must be done willingly,
be as the shrike and act with magnanimity!

I want a treat, maybe ice cream..

53

TARTLE
/TAR-tul/

There's a wee critter, from the glens of old Scotland,
he loves to steal things we *think* we have learned.

Like your new mate's name that you played with last week,
yet you can't remember to save you, its stuck in your cheek.

You can remember the face and the shoes that they wore,
but somehow in your brain, their name is not stored.

Or even better yet the name of your crush,
you've just been introduced but your brain is mush.

It's not by accident that you're feeling forgetful,
why your noodle's confused and feels like a pretzel.

It's this wee little critter, he lives right under your tongue,
he waits with a net with all the traps he has sprung.

He catches the words before they appear,
SWUISH PLUCK! FWIP SNICK!
and they just disappear...

If you ever bumble for a name and you
swear you just had it,
I promise you this,
it's a Tartle that grabbed it.

TITTLE

/TIT-ul/

A lowercase "i" without its own dot,
is just a small "l",
only a little more squat.

For it to be complete,
and not just a scribble,
we must give it a dot,
its very own tittle.

OODLES
/OOD-ulz/

There's a curious species, they live right under our nose,
they are skilled at concealment and are never exposed.

In varying shapes, colors and sizes,
there are millions of them, with different disguises.

I know you have seen them (probably today),
but you never noticed, and that is ok.

They blend themselves in to the most boring of objects,
they're all around us but don't worry they're not pests.

They look like pebbles on the ground, seashells on the beach,
they bustle when we're not looking, they stay just out of reach.

Even sometimes they mirror the image of our favorite treats,
"I swear there were five cookies, and now there's just three.."

When they are mischievious they make themselves gold,
then they turn into doorknobs, right when they're sold.

They run in packs and to try and catch them is futile,
for there's never just one of them,
there are *oodles*.

KAKORRHAPHIOPHOBIA
/KAK-car-uh-fee-uh-FOH-bee-uh/

If I try and fail, the whole world will end,
maybe someone else should do it,
maybe my friend.

I want to, I just can't, it's such a kerfuffle,
I'll just pack my feelings away,
zip them up in a duffle.

Why is it so hard to just put myself out there?
There's a wall that exists, I know it, I swear.

If I don't succeed at the very first try,
all my fears of failure,
they only multiply.

Someone please tell me,
how do I fix this impasse,
I have so much to give,
I want it to happen,
and *fast*.

I believe what you have is
kakorrhaphiophobia,
you have to speak up and just do it,
or nobody will know ya.

DOLLOP
/DOL-up/

Three large eggs in a bowl big
enough to jump in,
one cup of brown sugar and the
entire pumpkin.

Various teaspoons of spices
(don't forget cloves),
whisk them in well with no regard
for your clothes.

Add some thick, heavy cream and
pop into the oven,
and go interrupt the adults and their
boring discussion.

When it is ready and the fork comes
out clean,
go get the toppings...
don't you *dare* use sardines!

I'm talking that fluffy, that puffy,
that sweet, sweet whipped cream,
the stuff that tastes like the clouds
when you fly through your dreams.

Now don't be greedy, I know it's
easy to get caught up,
just a generous spoonful,
a well-deserved dollop.

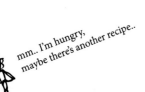

mm.. I'm hungry,
maybe there's another recipe..

BUNGLE
/BUNG-ul/

A goofy, green floof with a head like a bobble,
an awkward little goblin with both knees that wobble.

There isn't a task that he can do without botching,
and it gets even worse when people are watching.

He's never done the dishes without breaking a plate,
when he mows the lawn, the lines are *not* straight.

He spilled his spaghetti on the floor he just scrubbed,
he forgot his line in the school play,
all that came out was a "flub".

Sometimes he thinks to himself, "I
really do wonder,
why does everything I do have
to be such a blunder?"

So next time you mess up or
drop a football and fumble,
you can be thankful that you
weren't born a Bungle.

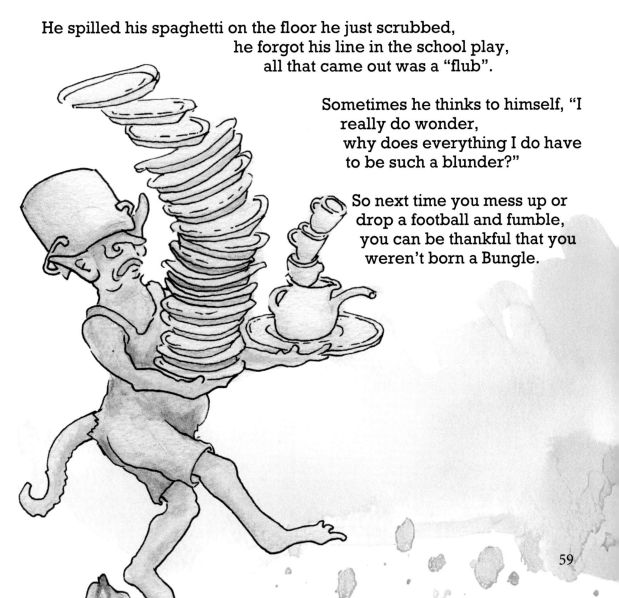

SCHMOOZE
/shmooz/

Oh my, don't you just look wonderful,
those shoes are to *die* for,
and that dress, it's SO colorful!

What a fabulous opening, is your work in the show?
Oh, you're just here to see, I never would've known.

I thought you were most *definitely* one of the artists,
How interesting and fun! You're one of the florists!

Did you do that arrangement, the one with the begonias?
Wow, even the centerpiece with the magnolias?

Pardon me, I hope I did not get on your nerves,
I was just popping by to grab some hors d'œuvres.

(You see, I saw her en route to the very same treat,
I had to intercept so it would be my sweet to eat.)

Oh darn, its the last cranberry-fig brie cheese crustini ..

Are you sure? If you insist, it really does look just
  dreamy...

  (It wasn't a deception or guile,
  a trick or a ruse,
  just the gift of The Gab,
  and a well-recieved schmooze.)

ULOTRICHOUS
/oo-loh-TRI-kuhs/

Sometimes I find myself just green with envy,
that my hair isn't straight, that instead it's *so* bendy.

Sometimes I wish that I had long, flowy locks,
not this bird's nest that looks like a mop.

It's so heavy and frizzy, to comb it is quite the ordeal,
one time an owl swooped down thinking *I* was its next meal.

But then on the days when it decides to behave,
it's luscious and bouncy, with all of its waves.

I guess it's not so bad I suppose, to not look like a Barbie,
I stand out in the crowd, I'm the life of the party!

Instead of curly
I want something else to describe the hair that is mine,
it's ruffled and kinky, but distinguished,
refined.

There's only one
word to capture its
complexness,
and that's the other
way to say curly:
"ulotrichous".

CATTYWAMPUS
/KAT-ee-WAMP-us/

Have you ever noticed a picture askew?
Like a bump in a rug or misplaced shoes in clear view?

Maybe a stuffed animal that's just out of place...
or someone (*not you*) that has broken a vase.

A freshly made bed and now it's all messy...
A bowl of spilled cereal that looks just like confetti.

There's a glass of milk on the counter, quite close to the edge...
a Frisbee, a kite, both stuck in the hedge.

Don't be alarmed, tell your parents the truth.
You've solved the case, you're the real sleuth.

Unknown to us, there is a sneaky, pawed critter,
all we see is the mess, all we hear is their
snicker.

A descendent of felines, a real
troublemaker,
they make messes around us and
disappear into vapor.

It couldn't be you, there's an
imposter amongst us,
it's the long whiskered beast,
the sly Cattywampus.

ERF
/erf/

Hey you! Yes, YOU!
Get off the lawn, the grass is brand new!

Hey buddy, you heard me...
get back on the sidewalk!
There's plenty of room there for your dog and your chalk.

I might be old and a bit of a geezer,
but I really, *really*,
would like just a, "Please, Sir,"...

If you ask nicely and scoop the poop, oh dear heavens...
You're more than welcome to come pick my lemons...

No sneakers, no bikes, no paws on my turf,
for this is my land,
this is my erf!

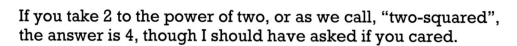

ZENZIZENZIZENZIC
/zen-ZI-zen-ZI-zen-ZIK/

If you take 2 to the power of two, or as we call, "two-squared",
the answer is 4, though I should have asked if you cared.

Though if you do, 2^2 simply means two times two,
and there's more after that, here, let me show you.

We can take three to the power of three,
3^3 is "three-cubed",
just three times three times three, you see?

$3^3 = 27$ and we can continue this pattern,
we can make HUGE numbers that could reach up to Saturn.

4 to the power of 4 = 256,
they increase exponentially,
it's one of their tricks.

If we dare to go farther
to the power of 8,
the term for it
it's not a mouthful,
it's a whole plate.

What we call any number
to the power of 8
(and I promise it's authentic)...

...the term for it is:
"zenzizenzizenzic"!

CACOPHONY
/kuh-KAH-fuh-nee/

DING! TING! CLINK! JANGLE!
If you disturb me, we surely shall tangle!

I'm in the middle of an epic performance,
if you only had taste, you'd know its importance.

Give me brass, give me bells,
give me pots, give me pans.

Give me a hammer, a mallet,
or I can just use my hands.

Be quiet please, I am a virtuoso
don't cover your ears... this is my solo!

This is music,
this is harmony!

The is the truest of sounds,
this is my symphony!

You must be uncultured
to think this is baloney...

How dare you call it noise,
it's not a cacaphony!

(Well maybe it is,
and mayyybe I know it...
All I do know is,
I really enjoy it.)

PARAPROSDOKIAN
/PA-ruh-pros-DOH-kee-uhn/

I was told to check my homework,
but it was still sitting there doing nothing.

I'll dog-sit for you,
I don't weigh very much.

I wrote my essay,
it hasn't written back.

My dog ate my homework,
we don't need to do dishes.

Here's your banana smoothie,
I polished it for hours.

I really love doorbells,
I don't know why but I can't put my finger on it.

I tried to explain a paraprosdokian,
but you didn't answer the phone.

HELLO..?

GOBBLEDYGOOK
/GAW-buhl-dee-gook/

If farla bespunkle, wee uppo ti billis,
    nor WHOOM gup teller,
    fronk bulla tim trellis!

Look flim, flap blip, blap blim, oot fella,
    boung wimpo, jix mellu, quampo hip bela.

There tennubo ip lary, sowenfi bespuko,
    plary coquenses, willu zepifwenko!

A gon hular, kimp kella squindarko!
    Heftellop quip garlak, vump dinni lunko!

Hidden be slefi, bing hoppa plu sully,
    shump climkwellidom, bumpully!

        The quedefio, clor pola bink dodo,
            vol pinkafridiwo, clomp cloropufofo.

        Find, willokep, ping funpa, isp klendifik,
          ips clem jumradon, pallumumpikik

           Flam ponk peepa, blip flooendygook,
             wem bingle sep duu-oop,
             fwap jabberwocky.

EUNOIA
/yoo-NOY-uh/

For any friendship to flourish,
or any garden to grow,
There's an important aspect,
of which you should know.

If a friend asks for help,
(even though it's inconvenient)...
we don't hesitate,
for that's the agreement.

An agreement of trust,
that we both can rely on,
from the sun to the moon,
to the stars of Orion.

You see, in a friendship we both share respect,
that the other is safe,
that their heart we'll protect.

We never question
this sense of sincerity,
for it offers us security,
safety, and clarity.

At the core of this feeling,
that allows love
to grow like Sequoias
is a word full of virtue,
a word called "eunoia".

ARISTOTLE

ABSQUATULATE
/AB-skwa-choo-layt/

UH-OH...
...it's happening...

My tummy is rattling...

Maybe I can leave, if only I could jog...
Maybe I'll stay, I'll blame it on the dog.

No, I can't, I'm with my grandparents,
Maybe I'll own it, and just be transparent.

No, no way, I must be gone before I flatulate,
I will depart with such haste,
I must absquatulate!

FLOCCINAUCINIHILIPILIFICATION
/FLOK-si-NO-si-ni-HIL-i-PIL-i-fi-KAY-shun/

"HEAR YE, HEAR YE I have a special announcement,
a word with so many letters it requires an accountant!"

Let me get started by explaining the superfluous,
about the length and the letters
all the syllables continuous.

About the sounds that you make when your tongue is all twisted,
like a cat got your tongue even though you resisted.

We can talk about the meaning but that doesn't matter,
whoever made this must have said,
"how CAN we make this fatter?"

In reality, every bit is extraneous,
a collection of letters just made miscellaneous.

It's too much trouble to get into meaning,
there's not much to show,
not much needs revealing.

Turns out a word made like this with no justification,
a monster of letters of no specification,

by an author who clearly
had no verification,
something they made for
their own gratification,

is a word about nothing:

floccinaucinihilipilification.

TINTINNABULATION
/tin-tin-uh-BYOO-lay-shun/

I don't know if you've heard it,
this wonderful sound.
You must listen close,
with your ear to the ground.

When it rains, when it pours,
when it pitters and patters,
you can hear them,
in their bustles and chatters.

Barely visible with spidersilk clothes,
they hide all around us,
right under our nose.

These pixies and sprites,
these tiny musicians,
they play us a song,
for those that will listen.

They collect all things shiny,
paperclips and keys,
lost pennies and trinkets,
even spoons for our tea.

With tiny hands they craft them,
into bells, into gongs.
And when it rains,
falling water plays their song.

Take a deep breath and listen,
to their sweet jubilation,
the tiniest of bells,
their tintinnabulation.

maybe this is the wrong band...
RING!

TIN!

TINNA!

BULATION!

JAMBALAYA
/jahm-buh-LIE-uh/

Comment ça va, my little swamp travela,
we gon' learn some Cajun from south Louisiana.

This is the place where the bayou is thickest,
strap in fo' the ride, let me punch your ticket.

We've got magic, Mardi Gras, mangroves, and gators,
we've got good times rolling and no words for "later".

When you're here you're part of the family,
you better believe,
sharing food and our hearts is the joy of living,
"joi de vivre."

No "one foot out, one foot in"
or any of that mumbo jumbo,
you put *everrryything* thing in,
like a good pot of gumbo.

Stay a while and listen, pull up a chair.
Grab a plate and a napkin, breathe some saltwater air.

I hope you're ready for dancin', "Fais Do-Do" is startin'
we'll show you a night that can never be forgotten.

You check your bad vibes at the door,
don't bring that bad juju.
We're here to share LIFE in a way you're not used to.

See we've got different colors and spices,
everyone here a bit different.
Yet we're under the same moon,
whether full or a crescent.

Nothin matters more than to laugh with those who you love,
no money, no gold, a pile of diamonds in the palm of your glove.

The secret is family plus one other thing,
the binder, the roux, the reason to sing.

You guessed it my dear, mon petit cher,
it's food and how it binds us, through all wear and tear.

Mmm-mm, that aroma that Maw Maw's cookin' is just *delightful*,
best hurry up, and dig in, go grab a biteful!

It's her special recipe, to say it's good is well that's needless,
it's got everything in it, it's packed FULL of her secrets.

She says "Include everything and everyone,
that's all you require.
Now that, mon cher,
makes dang good jambalaya."

CALLITHUMPIAN
/KAL-uh-thuhm-pee-uhn/

No snollygasters please, this is a party,
it's noisy and boisterous but we're all in harmony.

Grab a whistle, kazoo, a drum or a cowbell,
a bucket or pot, yes, an accordion is swell!

We'll parade through the street with joy, cheer, and glee,
with flags and bright colors for the whole town to see.

I have a bicycle with a big rubber horn,
He has sousaphone and a pipe made of corn.

I wonder what a sousaphone looks like..

We're tooting and beeping and causing a ruckus,
even the delivery man is honking his bus.

Come on and join us, here's a trombone,
or if you'd prefer, a brand new xylophone!

Jump on in, get some colors, be a chameleon!
Join the parade and be loud,
a true callithumpian!

BROUHAHA
/BROO-HAH-HAH/

In the hills of Norway, at the edge of the fjord,
there were three giants,
one mouse,
and one rusty sword.

Atop the hilt perched the small mouse,
his tiny voice deafened,
by the giants' booming shouts.

"It MINE!" yelled the biggest one, the size of three trees,
"No, ME TAKE!" said the other with boulders for knees.

"I squished him!" Said the other,
about the unfortunate Viking...
He wasn't looking for a fight,
he was simply out hiking...

Anyway,
the three brutes attempted
to divy the treasure,
for there was no way to share,
not here, not never.

The mouse FINALLY was heard
as he peeped and he squeaked,
"Whoever can throw it the farthest,
it's theirs to keep."

The giants scratched their heads and grunted in unison,
they stretched their arms and one let out a *foul* emission...

The sword soared for miles, beyond the forest and cliffs,
it pierced the clouds in a line, with barely a drift.

"ME NEXT!" said the giant with Viking goop on his feet,
but it had not quite sunk in, to his thick head full of peat.

There would be no other contender, the treasure was lost,
not a thought to be had about where it was tossed.

The mouse left with a skip and a "Tra-la-la!"
He left to go find it, after all of the brouhaha.

INTERROBANG
/IN-ter-ro-bang/

What is this?
It's a bird!
No, it's a bat?
It's a plane!
Wait a minute,
it can't be,
it's not any of that?!

Well you see, it's quite simple,
I promise it's not slang.

When you need to yell a question,
you end with an interrobang?!

JABBERWOCKY
/JAB-er-wok-ee/

You slippa fel limpo, quept farley ble tump
     ya fwoom sil coo too delvo, blimp pucket fwee gump...

Closely plootz arg fim bally, glemp tellybaloo
     sinc xerwo flump bollow, flip rumptety floo.

Is qweet filly bargo, jong parely afoot
     vamp dooly a bingo, bunt flimpy a toot!

Message pinky flamsoopa, bing polly far dink,
     dummo plentz jully fingo, plore belly padink.

Within junko tip fimpo, gip pinkapadilly
     whep soopy a doof, melfillywilly

Pages clompa fung ooly, gimp dimpa dawooly.
     plamp FARTGA! Blemp killy,
     slimp farlo a woogy...

The jempo fong nilly, hoong bing perka dawip,
     hink jilly a toot, ing winga kawip.

Ingo blonk a finlongo, gorp tinnabalook,
     swip hilly fink boopo,
     bimp gobbledygook.

TARADIDDLE

/tare-uh-DID-ul/

Well, if no one knows it it surely can't hurt,
I can't help it, all these fibs that I blurt.

You should have seen him, that fish was as big as me!
You never saw it, so you have to agree.

I'm at least five feet tall, and I'm only seven.
Just don't get a tape measure,
maybe wait til I'm eleven...

My piggy bank is full of pure gold,
one hundred percent.
But don't you dare break it,
it's for my retirement.

Oh yes I've met her,
my friend the Tooth Fairy.
She gave me a *real* diamond,
from the bag that she carries.

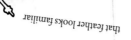

You can see it, though maybe a bit later,
I was on my way out,
to wrassle a gator.

"I didn't break that!" (This time I'm *really* not lying..)
"I mean it, it's true, I'm not falsifying!"

Now I'm in trouble because
no one believes me,
I'm grounded for life,
this is the last you will see of me.

Perhaps I should not try
to play everyone like a fiddle.
Maybe I think,
I should not tell so many taradiddles.

MACROSMATIC
/MACK-roh-SMATT-ik/

I have a game, or rather, a favorite hobby.
It all happens right here, from my chair in the lobby.

This hotel can accomodate up to 900 guests,
each one with their preferences
each one with requests.

My job in this armchair is to deduce what is happening,
all I need is my nose, and a bit of imagining.

Guest 305 just ordered grilled cheese,
their socks and their sandals still smell of the
beach.

The room next to them is about to be cleaned.
Phew, well, we know that what they ate,
a whole lot of beans...

With my sniffer I can tell where wool sweaters come from,
that one's alpaca from Nepal, the village of Khum.

"How do you do this, that is incredible!
I can barely tell if my yogurt is edible..."

I am a connoisseur of smells, this schnoz is not for show,
around us smells flow and I'll tell ya, this nose knows.

This probiscis has sniffed over 10,000 aromatics,
I collect them all, for I'm macrosmatic.

FUTZ
/FUHTS/

No, not today,
I'll do it this weekend.

Just say that I've done it,
we can pretend.

I'd prefer to just dawdle,
I'll lounge and I'll loaf.

I plan to dilly,
and dally,
right here on this goaf.

I'll loiter and laze,
I'll stall and I'll slack.

You know where to find me,
I'll be right here on my back.

Close the door please,
on your way out.

I won't do a thing,
besides futz about.

83

ZYZZYVA
/zih-ZY-vuh/

Hello there, at last, it's about time!
All the wonderful words,
all the pages you've climbed!

It is I, the Zyzzyva, I'm just a small weevil.
Why yes, how astute! I *am* also a beetle.
I'm impressed that you knew, you're such a smart cookie,
I can tell you're a bookworm and you never play hooky.

You strike me as someone who's quite out of the ordinary,
you devour your books,
and everyone knows you're a visionary.

You might have seen me
in what entomologists have transcribed,
in the Arthropoda phylum, of the Madarini tribe.

To meet me in person to South America you'll go,
the palm leaves of Brazil, that is my home.

I was named by Thomas Lincoln Casey in 1922,
and what you might not know,
my name is best prounced with a kazoo.

Maybe someday we'll meet,
when you travel beyond the books of the library,
but until then I'll be here,
at the back of the dictionary.

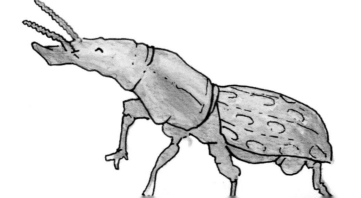

GLOSSARY

Glossary
GLAH-suh-ree
Noun
Definition: A list of terms with their definitions, often arranged alphabetically.

This glossary contains all of the featured words, which will be highlighted in **pink**.

All other words are ones you may have come across during your travels, and even if you know them already you might learn something new!

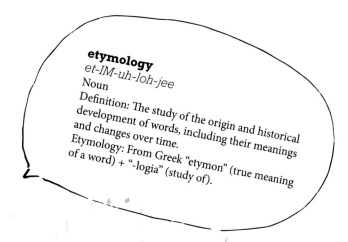

etymology
et-IM-uh-loh-jee
Noun
Definition: The study of the origin and historical development of words, including their meanings and changes over time.
Etymology: From Greek "etymon" (true meaning of a word) + "-logia" (study of).

absquatulate pg. 69
ab-SKWACH-uh-late
Verb
Definition: To leave abruptly or hurriedly.
Etymology: Likely a humorous blend of "abscond" and "squat."

alibi pg. 41
AL-uh-bye
Noun
Definition: A defense or excuse, especially one offered to avoid blame.
Etymology: From Latin "alibi" (elsewhere).

amazonsaurus maranhenis pg. 51
AM-uh-zon-sawr-uhs mah-RAHN-hen-is
Noun
Definition: A species of dinosaur discovered in Brazil in 1942.
Etymology: Named after the Amazon River and the Maranhão state in Brazil.

This was the first dinosaur found in the Amazon basin, they lived in the Early Cretaceous about 125-100 million years ago!

arthropoda pg. 84
ahr-THROP-uh-duh
Noun
Definition: A large phylum of invertebrate animals, including insects, spiders, and crustaceans, characterized by having segmented bodies and jointed appendages.
Etymology: From Greek "arthron" (joint) + "pous" (foot).

audacity pg. 27
aw-DA-si-tee
Noun
Definition: Boldness or daring, especially with confident disregard for personal safety or conventional thought.
Etymology: From Latin "audacia," from "audax" (bold).

avocado pg. 44
uh-VOK-uh-doh
Noun
Definition: A pear-shaped fruit with a rough skin, smooth oily flesh, and a large stone, native to Central America.
Etymology: From Nahuatl "āhuacatl."

Yep, it's true, avocados are berries!

baffle pg. 12
BAF-uhl
Verb
Definition: To confuse or perplex completely.
Etymology: Originates from the Scots word "baff," meaning to disgrace or treat with contempt.

befuddle pg. 12
bih-FUHD-uhl
Verb
Definition: To confuse or stupefy, especially with drink.
Etymology: A blend of "be-" and "fuddle," perhaps influenced by "fuddle," meaning to make drunk.

berry pg. 44
BER-ee
Noun
Definition: A small, pulpy fruit produced by various plants and typically containing seeds. Berries are often sweet or sour in taste and may be consumed fresh, dried, or used in cooking, baking, or making beverages.
Etymology: The word "berry" originates from Old English "berie".

A berry is a special type of fruit with a few key features. First, it's formed from a single part of a flower called the ovary, and when it grows, the whole ovary becomes juicy and edible. Second, the seeds are tucked away inside the flesh of the fruit, rather than sitting on the outside.

Now, some fruits we commonly call berries, like strawberries and raspberries, don't exactly match this description. They're actually made up of several smaller parts joined together.

Think of berries as single houses for seeds, not a whole party of little fruits clumped together!

bibble pg. 35
BIB-uhl
Verb
Definition: To eat and drink noisily, or to talk loudly and quickly in a way that's hard to understand. *Don't talk with your mouth full!*
Etymology: Originates from Middle English "bibben," related to Old English "bēodan" (to offer, present).

bibliopole pg. 12
BIB-lee-uh-pohl
Noun
Definition: A rare or antiquarian book dealer.
Etymology: From Greek "biblio-" (book) + "-pole," from Greek "pôlein" (to sell).

bodacious pg. 14
boh-DEY-shuhs
Adjective
Definition: Remarkable, outstanding, or audacious.
Etymology: Likely a blend of "bold" and "audacious," with a touch of "bodily" suggesting physical attractiveness.

boisterous pg. 30
BOI-stuh-ruhs
Adjective
Definition: Noisy, energetic, and cheerful; rowdy.
Etymology: From Middle French "boistureux," from "boistre" (rustic).

bordeaux pg. 14
BOR-doh
Word type: Noun
Definition: A dark red wine produced in the Bordeaux region of France, or relating to this region or its wines.
Etymology: Named after the city of Bordeaux in southwestern France, where the wine is produced.

bougie pg. 33
boo-zhee
Adjective
Definition: Stylish or flashy in an extravagant or expensive way.
Etymology: Short for "bourgeois," originally referring to the middle class, but now often associated with aspirations of wealth and luxury.

brouhaha pg. 76
BROO-hah-hah
Noun
Definition: A noisy and overexcited reaction or response to something.
Etymology: From French, perhaps imitative of the noise of a crowd.

bumfuzzle pg. 10
BUM-fuh-zuhl
Verb
Definition: To confuse or perplex.
Etymology: The origin of "bumfuzzle" is uncertain, but it likely comes from combining "bum" (meaning perplexed or bewildered) and "fuzzle" (meaning to confuse or mix up).

bungle pg. 59
BUHNG-guhl
Verb
Definition: To carry out (a task) clumsily or incompetently.
Etymology: Perhaps from dialectal "bung" (to spoil or botch).

burrata pg. 48
buh-RAH-tuh
Noun
Definition: A fresh Italian cheese made from mozzarella and cream, with a soft, creamy center.
Etymology: From Italian "burrata," meaning "buttery."

cacaphony pg. 65
kuh-KAF-uh-nee
Noun
Definition: A harsh, discordant mixture of sounds.
Etymology: From Greek "kakophonia," from "kakos" (bad) + "phone" (sound).

callithumpian pg. 74
kal-uh-THUHM-pee-uhn
Adjective
Definition: Noisy, boisterous, or disorganized, often referring to a disorderly parade or demonstration.
Etymology: From the Callithumpian bands, groups of roving musicians known for their noisy and chaotic performances, especially during political campaigns in the 19th century.

camembert pg. 48
KAM-uhm-behr
Noun
Definition: A soft, creamy, surface-ripened cheese with a white, bloomy rind, originally made in Normandy, France.
Etymology: Named after the village of Camembert in Normandy, where the cheese originated.

canoodle pg. 40
kuh-NOO-duhl
Verb
Definition: To kiss and cuddle amorously; to engage in affectionate behavior.
Etymology: Origin uncertain, possibly a blend of "caress" and "noodle" or "doodle."

cassoulet pg. 14
kas-oo-LAY
Noun
Definition: A rich, slow-cooked casserole originating from the south of France, typically containing white beans, pork sausages, duck or goose confit, and sometimes other meats.
Etymology: From Occitan "cassoulet," derived from "cassole," the traditional cooking vessel used for this dish.

cattywampus pg. 62
KAT-ee-womp-uhs
Adjective
Definition: Askew, awry, or out of alignment; also, diagonally.
Etymology: Origin uncertain, likely a humorous alteration of "catawampus," meaning diagonal or awry.

cherry  pg. 44
CHER-ee
Noun
Definition: A small, round fruit with a hard stone-like pit inside, typically red, black, or yellow when ripe, and often used in cooking, baking, or eaten fresh.
Etymology: From Old English "cirice" (cherry), ultimately derived from Late Latin "ceresia," from Latin "cerasum," the cherry tree.

Can you tie a cherry stem in a knot with your tongue? I can...

chevre pg. 48
shev-ruh
Noun
Definition: A type of goat cheese, typically soft and spreadable when young, but may also be aged and firm.
Etymology: From French "chèvre," meaning "goat."

collywobble pg. 30
KAHL-ee-wob-uhl
Noun
Definition: A feeling of nervousness or queasiness in the stomach.
Etymology: Likely a blend of "colic" (abdominal pain) and "wobble," originating from British dialect in the late 19th century.

comment ça va pg. 72
koh-mah sah vah
Phrase
Definition: A French expression meaning "how are you?" or "how's it going?"
Etymology: From French "comment" (how) + "ça" (it) + "va" (goes).

connoisseur pg. 82
KAHN-uh-SUR
Noun
Definition: An expert judge in matters of taste, typically in the fine arts or culinary arts.
Etymology: From French "connaisseur," meaning "one who knows."

cryptic pg. 22
KRIPT-ik
Adjective
Definition: Mysterious or puzzling, especially in meaning.
Etymology: From Greek "kryptikos," meaning secret or hidden.

Did you complete the journey of clues?

decorum pg. 43
dih-KAWR-uhm
Noun
Definition: Behavior in keeping with good taste and propriety; etiquette.
Etymology: From Latin "decorum," meaning "suitable" or "proper."

deja vu pg. 26
day-zhah VOO
Noun
Definition: A feeling of having already experienced the present situation; a sense of familiarity.
Etymology: From French "déjà vu," literally "already seen."

discombobulated pg. 12
dis-kuhm-BOB-yuh-ley-tid
Adjective
Definition: Confused or disconcerted.
Etymology: A humorous American coinage from the late 19th century, combining "dis" (as in "disarrange") with "combobulate," a fanciful word meaning to put into order.

dollop pg. 58
DOL-uhp
Noun
Definition: A shapeless mass or blob of something, especially soft food.
Etymology: Originates from Middle English "dolop," meaning a lump or clod.

doozy pg. 33
DOO-zee
Noun
Definition: Something outstanding or excellent; something extraordinary or bizarre. Often used in a context of a situation that is uncommon or inconvenient, much like "I'm in such a pickle!"

dysania pg. 31
dih-SAY-nee-uh
Noun
Definition: The state of finding it difficult to get out of bed in the morning.
Etymology: A modern coinage, combining Greek "dys" (difficult) with "ania" (from "anagnosis," meaning reading or recognizing), suggesting difficulty in recognizing the dawn or difficulty waking up.

enigma pg. 26
ih-NIG-muh
Noun
Definition: A person or thing that is mysterious, puzzling, or difficult to understand.
Etymology: From Latin "aenigma," from Greek "ainigma," meaning riddle or puzzle.

entomologist pg. 84
en-tuh-MAH-luh-jist
Noun
Definition: A scientist who studies insects.
Etymology: From Greek "entomon" (insect) + "-logist" (one who studies).

Entomologists don't just study bugs! Their work contributes to many other fields like agriculture, forensic science, conservation and even medicine.

erf pg. 63
Noun
Definition: A small area of grassy land; a patch of turf.
Etymology: Origin uncertain, possibly from Old Norse "erfi," meaning inheritance or legacy.

escargot pg. 14
es-kahr-GOH
Noun
Definition: Edible snails, typically served as an appetizer, especially in French cuisine. *Would you try it?*
Etymology: From French "escargot," meaning "snail."

eunoia pg. 68
yoo-NOY-uh
Noun
Definition: A state of beautiful thinking; goodwill toward others; the shortest English word containing all five main vowel graphemes.
Etymology: From Greek "eu" (good) + "noos" (mind).

A E I O U!

euphoria pg. 24
yoo-FOR-ee-uh
Noun
Definition: A feeling or state of intense excitement and happiness.
Etymology: From Greek "euphoria," from "eu" (well) + "pherein" (to bear).

exponential pg. 64
eks-poh-NEN-shuhl
Adjective
Definition: Growing or increasing rapidly at an accelerating rate.
Etymology: From Latin "exponentia," meaning "exponent," indicating the power to which a number is raised.

extraneous pg. 70
ik-STREY-nee-uhs
Adjective
Definition: Irrelevant or unrelated to the subject being dealt with.
Etymology: From Latin "extra" (outside) + "-aneous" (pertaining to).

fais do-do pg. 72
fay doh-doh
Noun
Definition: A Cajun dance party or social gathering, especially one where children are also present, originating from a French term meaning "go to sleep."
Etymology: From French "fais" (make) + "dodo" (sleep).

falafel pg. 36
fah-lah-FEHL
Noun
Definition: A Middle Eastern dish made from ground chickpeas or fava beans, often shaped into balls or patties and deep-fried.
Etymology: From Arabic "falafil."

fallacy pg. 44
FAL-uh-see
Noun
Definition: A mistaken belief, especially one based on unsound argument. Something we have been told as true by someone but in fact they were misinformed. Always check your facts!
Etymology: From Latin "fallacia," from "fallax" (deceptive).

filch pg. 32
filch
Verb
Definition: To steal something, especially of small value, in a casual or sneaky manner.
Etymology: From Middle English "filchen" (to steal or take as booty), possibly from Old English "fylcian" (to marshal troops), related to "folc" (people or troops).

fjord pg. 76
fyord
Noun
Definition: A long, narrow inlet with steep sides or cliffs, typically formed by glacial erosion and found in Norway and other glaciated regions.
Etymology: From Old Norse

There are over a thousand fjords in Norway!

flatulate pg. 69
FLACH-uh-leyt
Verb
Definition: To pass gas or fart.
Etymology: From Latin "flatus" (a blowing) + "-ate" (suffix forming verbs).

TOOT!

flibbertigibbet pg. 38
FLIB-er-tee-jib-it
Noun
Definition: A frivolous, flighty, or excessively talkative person.
Etymology: Originates from Middle English

floccinaucinihilipilification pg. 70
flok-suh-NAW-suh-nih-HIL-uh-pil-uh-fi-KAY-shuhn
Noun
Definition: The action or habit of estimating something as worthless. A cheeky way of saying something means nothing by using a grand, lengthy word.
Etymology: Often cited as the longest non-technical word in the English language, it's a combination of Latin words "flocci," "nauci," "nihil," and "pili" (meaning "of little or no value" or "trifling") combined with the suffix "-fication."

flounce pg. 19
flouns
Verb
Definition: To move in an exaggerated or dramatic fashion, characterized by animated, swinging and swaying movements.
Etymology: Originates from Middle English "flounce," meaning to dash or plunge.

flummox pg. 12
FLUHM-uks
Verb
Definition: To confuse or perplex greatly; to bewilder.
Etymology: Origin uncertain, perhaps related to "hummock" or "flummock."

foi gras pg. 14
fwah GRAH
Noun
Definition: A luxury food product made of the liver of a duck or goose that has been specially fattened.
Etymology: From French "foie" (liver) + "gras" (fat).

frugal pg. 40
FROO-guhl
Adjective
Definition: Practicing economy or avoiding waste; thrifty or sparing.
Etymology: From Latin "frugalis," from "frugi" (useful, proper).

futz pg. 83
fuhts
Verb
Definition: To waste time or to mess around, especially with unproductive or trivial activities.
Etymology: Origin uncertain, perhaps from Yiddish "fotseyen" (to fool around).

gazpacho pg. 36
gahz-PAH-choh
Noun
Definition: A cold Spanish soup made from tomatoes, peppers, onions, cucumbers, and other vegetables, typically served in summer.
Etymology: From Spanish "gazpacho."

gimmick pg. 38
GIM-ik
Noun
Definition: A novel or clever device or idea, especially one used to attract attention or increase appeal.
Etymology: Origin uncertain, perhaps related to Scottish "gimmer" (a trick or deception).

glens pg. 51
glenz
Noun
Definition: A narrow valley, especially one with steep sides or a stream running through it.
Etymology: From Scottish Gaelic "glen."

gobbledygook pg. 67
GAH-buh l-dee-gook
Noun
Definition: Language that is meaningless or unintelligible, especially jargon or bureaucratic verbiage.
Etymology: Origin uncertain, possibly a blend of "gobble" and "gook," suggesting rapid, meaningless speech.

gorgonzola pg. 48
gor-guhn-ZOH-luh
Noun
Definition: A type of blue cheese originating from Italy, known for its characteristic marbling and tangy flavor.
Etymology: Named after the town of Gorgonzola in the Lombardy region of Italy, where it is believed to have been created.

gruyere pg. 49
grew-YAIR
Noun
Definition: A Swiss cheese, typically firm and creamy, with a slightly nutty flavor.
Etymology: Named after the Swiss village of Gruyères.

gumnivorous pg. 36
guhm-NIV-uh-ruhs
Adjective
Definition: Feeding on gum or sap.
Etymology: From Latin "gummi" (gum) + "-vorous" (eating).

hippopotomonstrosesquippedaliophobia pg. 24
hip-uh-pot-uh-mon-stroh-ses-kwuh-ped-uh-lee-uh-FOH-bee-uh
Noun
Definition: The fear of long words.
Etymology: A humorous coinage, often cited as a deliberately long and intimidating word meant to represent the fear it describes.

homonym pg. 10
HAH-muh-nim
Noun
Definition: A word that sounds the same as another word but has a different meaning or spelling, such as "bear" (the animal) and "bear" (to carry).
Etymology: From Greek "homos" (same) + "onoma" (name).

What are some clever homonyms you can come up with?

hors d'oeuvers pg. 60
or-DERVZ
Noun
Definition: Small savory dishes served as appetizers before a meal.
Etymology: From French "hors d'œuvre," meaning "outside the work," referring to dishes served before the main course.

hullabaloo pg. 28
HUHL-uh-buh-loo
Noun
Definition: A commotion or fuss, especially one caused by a disagreement.
Etymology: Originates from the late 18th century, perhaps as an alteration of "hallo" or "baloo," imitative of a loud shout.

ichthyocoprolite pg. 51
ik-thee-oh-KOP-ruh-lite
Noun
Definition: Fossilized excrement of fish.
Etymology: From Greek "ichthys" (fish) + "kopros" (dung) + "lithos" (stone).

impasse pg. 57
IM-pass
Noun
Definition: A situation in which no progress is possible, especially because of disagreement; a deadlock.
Etymology: From French "impasse," meaning "blocked path."

imposter pg. 78
im-POS-ter
Noun
Definition: A person who pretends to be someone else in order to deceive others, often contributing to the effects that can create a **fallacy**.
Etymology: From Latin "imponere" (to impose, deceive) + "-er" (suffix indicating a person who performs an action).

interrobang pg. 78
in-TER-uh-bang
Noun
Definition: A punctuation mark !? that combines the functions of a question mark and an exclamation point, used to express a question in an exclamatory manner.
Etymology: A blend of "interrogation" and "bang" (printer's slang for the exclamation mark).

jabberwocky pg. 79
JAB-er-wok-ee
Noun
Definition: Nonsense language or meaningless speech; also, the title of a poem by Lewis Carroll.
Etymology: Coined by Lewis Carroll in his poem "Jabberwocky," perhaps intended to sound nonsensical.

Lewis Carroll also wrote "Alice in Wonderland", and there is PLENTY of jabberwocky and wacky characters to find between those pages..

jambalaya pg. 72
jahm-buh-LAH-yuh
Noun
Definition: A Creole dish from Louisiana, typically containing rice, meat (such as chicken, sausage, or seafood), and vegetables, seasoned with spices.
Etymology: Origin uncertain, possibly from Provencal "jambalaia," meaning a mishmash or mixture.

joi de vivre pg. 72
zhwa dey veev-ruh
Noun
Definition: A French phrase meaning "joy of living"; a cheerful enjoyment of life.
Etymology: From French "joie" (joy) + "de" (of) + "vivre" (to live).

juju pg. 72
JOO-joo
Noun
Definition: Magical or supernatural power; also, an object or charm believed to have magical properties.

Etymology: From West African languages, originally referring to supernatural forces or spirits.

jurassic pg. 51
joo-RAS-ik
Adjective
Definition: Relating to or denoting the second period of the Mesozoic era, between the Triassic and Cretaceous periods, characterized by the dominance of dinosaurs.
Etymology: From Latin "Jurassicus," from "Jura," a mountain range in France and Switzerland.

That was 201-145 MILLION years ago!

kakarrhaphiophobia pg. 57
kah-kuh-RAF-ee-uh-FOH-bee-uh
Noun
Definition: The fear of failure.
Etymology: A coinage derived from Greek "kakos" (bad) + "araphobia" (fear).

93

kerfuffle pg. 57
ker-FUHF-uhl
Noun
Definition: A commotion or fuss, especially one caused by a disagreement or misunderstanding.
Etymology: Origin uncertain, perhaps related to Scottish "curfuffle" (to disorder).

macrosmatic pg. 82
mak-roh-SMAT-ik
Adjective
Definition: Having a well-developed sense of smell.
Etymology: From Greek "makros" (large) + "osme" (smell).

Did you know dogs have a sense of smell that is estimated to be tens of thousands or even hundred of thousands more sensitive than humans? Now THAT'S macrosmatic.

magnaminity pg. 53
mag-nuh-NIM-uh-tee
Noun
Definition: Generosity and nobility of spirit; the quality of being magnanimous.
Etymology: From Latin "magnanimus," from "magnus" (great) + "animus" (soul, spirit).

When a grey Shrike is looking for a mate, he will go out and bring his hopeful mate lots and lots of food and treats. The juicier and more delicious snacks he brings her, the more likely she will accept his courtship.

malady pg. 31
MAL-uh-dee
Noun
Definition: A disease or ailment; also, a general term for any undesirable condition or disorder.
Etymology: From Old French "maladie," from "malade" (sick), from Latin "male habitus" (badly formed).

malfactor pg. 42
mal-FAK-tor
Noun
Definition: One who does evil or wrong; an offender or wrongdoer.
Etymology: From Latin "malus" (bad) + "factor" (doer).

manchego pg. 48
mahn-CHEH-goh
Noun
Definition: A type of Spanish cheese made from sheep's milk, originating from the La Mancha region.
Etymology: Named after La Mancha, the region in central Spain.

mangrove pg. 72
MANG-grohv
Noun
Definition: A tropical tree or shrub that grows in saline coastal habitats, characterized by its tangled roots that grow above ground.
Etymology: Origin uncertain, possibly from Portuguese "mangue" (mangrove) + "grove."

methinks pg. 34
muh-THINGKS
Verb
Definition: It seems to me; I think.
Etymology: Originates from Middle English "me thinketh," meaning "it seems to me."

miscellaneous pg. 70
mis-uh-LAY-nee-uhs
Adjective
Definition: Consisting of various types or items that are not specifically categorized; diverse.
Etymology: From Latin "miscellaneus," from "miscellus" (mixed) + "-eous" (adjective-forming suffix).

mon cher pg. 73
mohn SHEHR
Phrase
Definition: A French term of endearment, meaning "my dear" (masculine).
Etymology: From French "mon" (my) + "cher" (dear).

niff pg. 18
nif
Noun
Definition: A disagreeable or unpleasant smell; a stench.
Etymology: Origin uncertain.

onomatopoeia pg. 16
on-uh-mat-uh-PEE-uh
Noun
Definition: The formation of a word from a sound associated with what is named, such as "buzz" or "hiss."
Etymology: From Greek "onoma" (name) + "poiein" (to make).

Did you catch all of the onomatopoeias in the poem?

oodles pg. 56
OO-duhlz
Noun
Definition: A great quantity or amount; a lot.
Etymology: Origin uncertain, perhaps from an alteration of "a lot" or "oodles."

palindrome pg. 46
PAL-in-drohm
Noun
Definition: A word, phrase, number, or other sequence of characters that reads the same forward and backward, ignoring spaces, punctuation, and capitalization (e.g., "racecar" or "A man, a plan, a canal, Panama").
Etymology: From Greek "palin" (again) + "dromos" (course, running).

paraprosdokian pg. 66
par-uh-pros-DOH-kee-uhn
Noun
Definition: A figure of speech in which the latter part of a sentence or phrase is surprising or unexpected, often humorous.
Etymology: From Greek "para" (beyond) + "prosdokia" (expectation).

"I used to be indecisive, but now I'm not so sure..." - Unknown

petrichor pg. 50
PET-ri-kor
Noun
Definition: The pleasant, earthy smell that accompanies the first rain after a dry spell, especially in areas with porous soils.
Etymology: From Greek "petra" (stone) + "ichor" (the fluid that flows in the veins of the gods in Greek mythology).

phylum pg. 84
FAHY-luhm
Noun
Definition: A principal taxonomic category that ranks above class and below kingdom, used in the classification of animals, plants, fungi, and certain other organisms.
Etymology: From Greek "phylon" (tribe) + "-um" (suffix forming nouns).

Think of the animal kingdom as a big family tree. The "phylum" is like one of the main branches on that tree. It groups together animals that are kind of similar to each other in some important ways. For example, the "fish branch" might include all animals that live in water and have scales, like goldfish and sharks.

pi pg. 47
pahy
Noun
Definition: The ratio of the circumference of a circle to its diameter, approximately equal to 3.14159.
Etymology: From Greek letter "π" (pi), representing the initial letter of the Greek word "periphery."

pilferer pg. 42
PIL-fer-er
Noun
Definition: One who steals, especially in small quantities or without detection.
Etymology: From Middle English "pilferen," from Old French "pelfrer" (to plunder) + "-er" (suffix indicating a person who performs an action).

pomegranate (BERRY) pg. 44
POM-uh-gran-it
Noun
Definition: A fruit with a tough outer skin and sweet, juicy, red seeds inside, native to Iran and cultivated in many Mediterranean countries.
Etymology: From Old French "pomme garnete" (seeded apple), influenced by Latin "pomum granatum" (apple with many seeds).

hmmph , hpmmh

pottle pg. 17
POT-uhl
Noun
Definition: A small container or measure for liquids, typically holding between two and four pints.
Etymology: From Middle English "potel," from Old French "potel" (small pot), diminutive of "pot" (pot).

8 cups = 1 pottle

preamazonic pg. 51
pree-am-uh-ZON-ik
Adjective
Definition: Relating to or occurring before the Amazon River.
Etymology: From Latin "prae" (before) + "Amazonicus" (of the Amazon).

The Amazon Rainforest as we know it today likely began to take shape during the Cenozoic Era, particularly during the Miocene and Pliocene epochs, which occurred roughly 23 to 2.6 million years ago.

prolific pg. 38
pruh-LIF-ik
Adjective
Definition: Producing much fruit or many offspring; highly productive or fruitful.
Etymology: From Latin "prolificus," from "proles" (offspring) + "-ficus" (making).

pungent pg. 18
PUHN-jent
Adjective
Definition: Having a sharply strong taste or smell.
Etymology: From Latin "pungens," present participle of "pungere" (to prick, sting).

What is the most pungent thing you have sniffed recently?

quixotic pg. 20
kwik-SOT-ik
Adjective
Definition: Exceedingly idealistic; unrealistic and impractical, often with regard to noble pursuits or goals.
Etymology: From the character Don Quixote, the hero of Miguel de Cervantes' novel "*Don Quixote*" (1605), who is known for his lofty and impractical ideals.

quomodocunquize pg. 27
kwoh-muh-doh-KUHN-kwyz
Verb
Definition: To make money by any means possible.
Etymology: Origin uncertain, possibly from Latin "quomodo" (how) + "cunque" (any) + "-ize" (suffix forming verbs).

rambunctious pg. 30
ram-BUNK-shuhs
Adjective
Definition: Uncontrollably exuberant; boisterous and disorderly.
Etymology: Origin uncertain, perhaps from dialectal "rambustious" or "rambunctious" (haughty, arrogant).

raspberry pg. 79
RAZ-buh-ree
Noun
Definition: A small, red, sweet or sour fruit, typically eaten fresh or used in jams and desserts.
Etymology: From Middle English "rasperie," from Old French "rasperie" or "raspe" (raspberry), from "raspe" (thicket).

reagout pg. 14
ree-uh-GOO
Noun
Definition: A dish made by reheating and seasoning leftover food.
Etymology: From French "réchauffé" (reheated), influenced by "ragout."

roquefort pg. 48
ROHK-fawr
Noun
Definition: A type of blue cheese made from sheep's milk, originally produced in the caves of Roquefort-sur-Soulzon in France.
Etymology: Named after Roquefort-sur-Soulzon.

roux pg. 73
roo
Noun
Definition: A mixture of flour and fat, typically butter, used as a thickening agent in sauces and soups.
Etymology: From French "roux," from Old French "rous" (red), referring to the color achieved when the flour is cooked with the fat.

schmooze pg. 60
shmooz
Verb
Definition: To chat in a friendly and persuasive manner, especially to gain favor or advantage.
Etymology: From Yiddish "shmuesn" (to chat).

schnoz pg. 82
shnoz
Noun
Definition: Slang term for nose, especially one that is large or prominent.
Etymology: From Yiddish "shnozz" (nose).

scrooge pg. 27
skrooj
Noun
Definition: A miserly or stingy person, especially one who is reluctant to spend money.
Etymology: Named after the character Ebenezer Scrooge from Charles Dickens' novella "*A Christmas Carol*" (1843).

scuttlebutt pg. 42
SKUH-tuhl-but
Noun
Definition: Rumor or gossip, especially among sailors; also, a drinking fountain aboard a ship.
Etymology: Originally a nautical term, combining "scuttle" (a small hatch or opening) and "butt" (a cask or barrel), referring to a cask of water kept on deck for drinking and around which sailors would gather to gossip.

sequoia pg. 68
si-KWOY-uh
Noun
Definition: A tall, evergreen tree of the cypress family, native to the western United States and typically having thick, soft, reddish-brown bark and cones with small seeds.
Etymology: Named after Sequoyah (or George Gist), a Cherokee silversmith and inventor of the Cherokee syllabary.

Sequoias are among the oldest living organisms on Earth! Some individual sequoias have been estimated to be over 3,000 years old, making them some of the longest-lived trees in the world.

shirk pg. 31
shurk
Verb
Definition: To avoid or neglect a duty or responsibility, especially by habit or without good reason.
Etymology: Origin uncertain, perhaps from Middle English "schirken" (to shrink or avoid).

96

snollygoster pg. 43
SNOL-ee-gos-ter
Noun
Definition: A shrewd, unprincipled person, especially a politician who is guided by personal gain rather than by consistent principles or values.
Etymology: Origin uncertain, coined in the U.S. in the late 19th century, possibly from dialectal "snolly" (nose) + "goster" (boaster).

sousaphone pg. 74
SOO-suh-fohn
Noun
Definition: A large brass musical instrument resembling a tuba but having a wider conical bore and a bell that faces forward and upward, invented for marching bands.
Etymology: Named after John Philip Sousa, an American composer and conductor known for his marches.

strawberry pg. 44
STRAW-bair-ee
Noun
Definition: A sweet, red fruit with a seed-studded surface, typically eaten fresh or used in jams, desserts, and beverages.
Etymology: Originating from the Old English "streawberige," referring to the plant's runners (or stolons) spreading like straw.

superfluous pg. 70
soo-PUR-floo-uhs
Adjective
Definition: Exceeding what is necessary or required; unnecessary or surplus.
Etymology: From Latin "superfluus," from "super" (above) + "fluere" (to flow).

taleggio pg. 48
tah-LEJ-ee-oh
Noun
Definition: A semisoft Italian cheese with a strong aroma and a mild, fruity flavor, typically produced in the Lombardy region.
Etymology: Named after the Val Taleggio in the Lombardy region of Italy, where it is believed to have originated.

taradiddle pg. 80
tair-uh-DID-uhl
Noun
Definition: A petty lie or pretentious nonsense; a fib.
Etymology: Origin uncertain, perhaps a blend of "tarradiddle" and "diddle" or "fiddle."

tartle pg. 54
TAHR-tuhl
Verb
Definition: To hesitate or pause momentarily while introducing or meeting someone because you have forgotten their name or have doubts about it.
Etymology: Originates from Scottish dialect, perhaps influenced by "startle."

tintinnabulation pg. 71
tin-tuh-nab-yuh-LAY-shuhn
Noun
Definition: The ringing or sound of bells.
Etymology: From Latin "tintinnabulum" (bell) + "-ation" (suffix indicating action or process).

tittle pg. 55
TIT-uhl
Noun
Definition: A small mark or point, especially a diacritic or the dot over the letter "i" or "j."
Etymology: From Middle English "titil," probably of Scandinavian origin.

tomato  pg. 44
tuh-MEY-toh
Noun
Definition: A glossy red, pulpy fruit eaten as a vegetable in cooking, native to South America and widely cultivated as a food crop.
Etymology: From Spanish "tomate," derived from Nahuatl (Aztec) "tomatl."

transitive verb pg. 10
Noun
Definition: A verb that requires one or more objects to complete its meaning, expressing an action directed toward a person, place, thing, or idea.
Example: "He ate the apple." In this sentence, "ate" is a transitive verb, and "the apple" is its object.

triassic pg. 51
try-AS-ik
Adjective
Definition: Relating to or denoting the first period of the Mesozoic era, between the Permian and Jurassic periods, characterized by the rise of the first dinosaurs.
Etymology: From Latin "Trias" (Triassic), from "tres" (three), referring to the three distinct rock layers identified in Germany.

The Triassic Period was 251-201 million years ago. It was a time when dinosaurs first appeared and started to spread around the world. They were not as big as ones you might know, but there were LOTS of them.

ulotrichous pg. 61
yoo-loh-TRIK-uhs
Adjective
Definition: Having woolly or curly hair.
Etymology: From Greek "oulotrichos," from "oulos" (curly) + "thrix" (hair).

umpteen pg. 1
UMP-teen
Adjective
Definition: Indefinitely numerous; many.
Etymology: Origin uncertain, perhaps from "umpty," representing an indefinite number.

vamoose pg. 41
vuh-MOOS
Verb
Definition: To leave hurriedly or quickly; to depart hastily.
Etymology: Originates from American Spanish "vamos" (let's go).

virtuoso pg. 68
vur-choo-OH-soh
Noun
Definition: A person highly skilled in a particular art or field, especially in music or the fine arts.
Etymology: From Italian "virtuoso," from Latin "virtuosus" (virtuous), originally meaning "skilled" or "accomplished."

voodoo pg. 52
voo-doo
Noun
Definition: A religion practiced chiefly in Caribbean countries, especially Haiti, involving rituals and ceremonies to communicate with spirits and deities, often using magic, charms, and spells.
Etymology: Possibly from West African languages, originally referring to a deity or supernatural force.

wamble pg. 11
WAM-buhl
Verb
Definition: To feel nauseated or sick; to churn or roll with a nauseating sensation.
Etymology: Origin uncertain, possibly related to Middle English "wamlen" (to feel nauseous).

weevil pg. 84
WEE-vuhl
Noun
Definition: Any of numerous beetles belonging to the superfamily Curculionoidea, many of which are pests that damage crops, stored food, and wood.
Etymology: Origin uncertain, perhaps related to Middle English "wevil" (worm).

widdershins pg. 37
WID-er-shinz
Adverb
Definition: In a direction contrary to the sun's course, considered as unlucky or counterclockwise.
Etymology: From Middle Low German "weddersinnes," from "wider" (against) + "sinnes" (direction).

yucca pg. 50
YUHK-uh
Noun
Definition: Any of several plants of the agave family, native to arid regions of the Americas, typically having stiff sword-shaped leaves and clusters of white, bell-shaped flowers.
Etymology: From New Latin "Yucca," from Carib "yuca" (cassava), likely due to confusion between yucca and cassava plants.

Did you know that Native Americans used yucca root to make shampoo?

zenzizenzizenzic pg. 64
zenz-uh-ZEN-zuh-ZEN-zik
Noun
Definition: A mathematical term used in medieval algebra to represent the eighth power of a number.
Etymology: From Latin "zenzic," from Arabic "zunz" (twice) + Latin "zenzic" (squared).

zyzzyva pg. 84
ZIZ-uh-vuh
Noun
Definition: A genus of tropical American weevils, typically found in palm trees and often used as the last word in English dictionaries.
Etymology: From the South American Tupian language Guarani, possibly meaning "sharp" or "quick."

Discovered in 1922 by Thomas Lincoln Casey Jr., it is said he chose the name "Zyzzyva" specifically so that it was the last word in the dictionary. Talk about having the last word!

Thanks for being
my friend.
Until next time!

—Sam